For Jake Berube

It's a mouse.

It's a jackass.

LANE SMITH

It's a

Book

It's a monkey.

MACMILLAN CHILDREN'S BOOKS

What do you
have there?

It's a book.

How do you
scroll down?

I don't.
I turn the page.
It's a book.

Where's your mouse?

Can you
make the
characters
fight?

Nope.
Book.

Can it text?

No.

Tweet?

No.

Wi-Fi?

No.

Can it do this?

No...

it's a book.

Look.

"**Arrrrrrrr,**" nodded Long John Silver, "we're in agreement then?" He unsheathed his broad cutlass laughing a maniacal laugh, "Ha! Ha! Ha!" Jim was petrified. The end was upon him. Then in the distance, a ship! A wide smile played across the lad's face.

Too many letters.

I'll fix it.

So . . .

what else can this book do?

Does it need
a password?

No.

Need a
screen
name?

No.

It's a book.

Are you going
to give my
book back?

No.

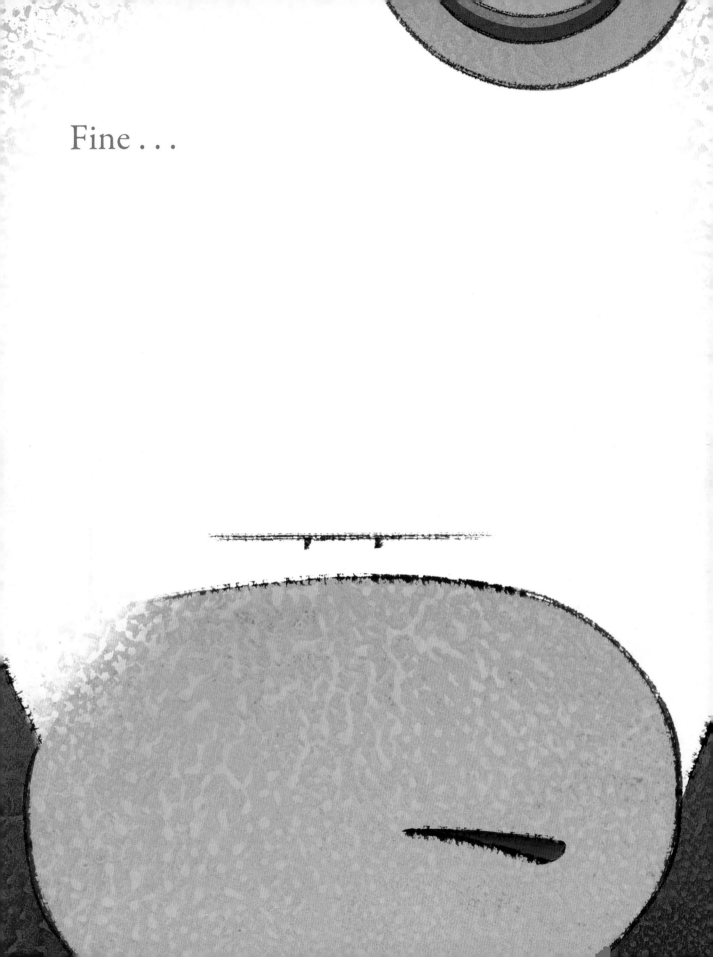

Fine . . .

I'm going to the library.

Don't worry, I'll charge
it up when I'm done!

You don't have to . . .

IT'S A BOOK, JACKASS.

LANE SMITH wrote a **BOOK** that was a *New York Times* best seller[1]. His illustrations in a **BOOK** won a Caldecott Honor Medal[2]. He wrote and illustrated a **BOOK** that was on many "best book" lists including *School Library Journal, The Horn Book, Publishers Weekly, Parenting* and *Child* magazines, and was a *New York Times* Best Illustrated Book of the Year[3]. He painted the pictures in a **BOOK** that sold millions of copies[4]. He created artwork in a **BOOK** by Roald Dahl and a **BOOK** by Florence Parry Heide and a **BOOK** by Dr. Seuss and Jack Prelutsky[5].

He is married to Molly Leach who designed all of the above **BOOKS**.

[1] *Madam President* [2] *The Stinky Cheese Man and Other Fairly Stupid Tales* written by Jon Scieszka [3] *John, Paul, George & Ben* [4] *The True Story of the Three Little Pigs* written by Jon Scieszka [5] *James and the Giant Peach, Princess Hyacinth (The Surprising Tale of a Girl Who Floated), Hooray for Diffendoofer Day!*

www.lanesmithbooks.com

First published in the USA 2010 by Roaring Brook Press
This edition published 2011 by Macmillan Children's Books
a division of Macmillan Publishers Limited
20 New Wharf Road, London N1 9RR
Basingstoke and Oxford
Associated companies throughout the world
www.panmacmillan.com

ISBN: 978-0-230-75313-6

Text and illustrations copyright © Lane Smith 2010
Book design by Molly Leach
Moral rights asserted.

A CIP catalogue record for this book is available from the British Library.

Printed in Belgium

The inclusion of author website addresses in this book does not constitute an endorsement by or an association with Macmillan Publishers of such sites or the content, products, advertising or other materials presented on such sites.

10 9 8 7 6 5 4 3 2 1